LET'S GO ALL AROUND THE NEIGHBORHOOD

By
PATTY THOMAS

Illustrated by
ANTHONY RAO

GOLDEN PRESS • NEW YORK
Western Publishing Company, Inc., Racine, Wisconsin

Susie and Mommy have lots of places to go today. They have errands to do all around the neighborhood.

"Let's go," says Mommy right after breakfast.

Susie and Mommy go to the post office.
They buy some stamps and mail a letter
to Aunt Nancy.

They go to Mr. Miller's shoe store.
Mommy buys Susie new red sneakers.

Susie wears her new sneakers
to the playground.
"See how fast I can run, Mommy!"
she calls.
Mommy pushes Susie
high in the swing.

Then Susie climbs the monkey bars,
all by herself.

"Let's have a special lunch today," Mommy says. So they go to a restaurant.

Susie has a hamburger with a pickle
and a glass of milk.

Mommy has a turkey sandwich and iced tea.

After lunch they go to the library.
The librarian helps them find the books
they want—two for Susie and two for Mommy.

LIBRARY

MON. 10:00
TUES. 10:
WED. 12

Outside the laundromat, Mommy gives Susie
a dime for the toy machine.
"Look, Mommy," says Susie. "I got a silver ring!"

At the hardware store, Mommy buys an eggbeater.
"We'll make muffins when we get home,"
she tells Susie. "You can help me beat the eggs."

Then they hurry to meet David at school.

On the way home,
they stop at Mrs. Peterson's
fruit-and-vegetable stand.

Mommy buys broccoli and carrots for dinner.
"And here's a nice apple for Susie,
and one for David," says Mrs. Peterson.
"Thank you," say Susie and David.

When they turn the corner,
they see Daddy at the bus stop.
Susie and David run to meet him.

Daddy has a hug and a kiss for each of them.

"Where are we going now?" Susie asks.
"The best place in the whole neighborhood,"
says Mommy. "Home."